THE
Alabama
Angels

By Mary Barwick

With Illustrations by the Author

The Black Belt Press
Montgomery, Alabama

It is dedicated to the spirit of love within us all and to my family who has given me "roots and wings."

Published by The Black Belt Press
Black Belt Communications Group
P.O. Box 551
Montgomery, AL 36101
(205) 265-6753

Design and Composition by Randall Williams
and Cindy Noe

FOURTH PRINTING, OCTOBER 1990

Printed in the United States of America by
Wells Printing Co., Montgomery, Alabama
Color separations by
Color Craft, Inc., Montgomery, Alabama

Set in Adobe Palatino on an Apple Macintosh
using Microsoft Word and Aldus PageMaker. All
trademarks acknowledged.

ISBN 0-9622815-1-4

THE
Alabama
Angels

IT WAS a crisp fall night in Alabama. Wisps of smoke curled from the chimney of the tidy cabin. The velvet sky held a sliver of moon and myriad stars. The cotton was high in the fields and the livestock slept peacefully.

Alethea knelt by her old shiny brass bed, with the treasured quilt her Mama had made, praying her best to a God she wasn't sure was there.

"Please, if you're listening, help my Mama and Daddy. They are fine folks. They work so hard and they're always talking about you; like you're friends. If you're still listening, they sure could use help. The cotton needs tendin', there's washin', ironin', animals to be fed, and Lord, all kinds of things to be doin'. My Mama says there aren't enough hours in the day. Could you manage a few more? Thank you, goodnight."

The Lord was listening as He always does and He smiled. Alethea wasn't the only one asking for that lately. He thought for a minute and He knew how He could help His good children who worked hard and cared for each other.

He sent for Bubba, who was one of his special angels reserved for Southern assignments. Bubba came flying. "Yes, Lord, you wanted me?"

"Bubba, I have a problem with my Alabama folks. They have more chores than they have hours in the day. Do you think you could round up some Southern angels and go to Alabama and help out during the night, lightening the load of those grand folks?"

"Oh, yes, Lord, I'll get Sara, Emily and some others and we'll be back in Heaven before the rooster crows."

Bubba, Sara and Emily's first stop was Alethea's house. They peeked in on her and her sisters as they slept.

Then they went to pick the cotton, wash some clothes, and rock the baby. They left just in time to beat the sun.

On their return the Lord was so pleased with their errand that He gave them their next assignment. It was to deliver a cow to a family in Selma. Theirs had been struck by lightning and five little children were depending on its milk. They had just asked the Lord to help them.

When the Alabama angels got home the Lord hugged them. His people were thanking Him more than ever.

Bubba and the others could hardly wait to see what the Lord had in store for them next. It was so exciting traveling from Mobile to Gadsden, from east to west. They even helped an aging stork deliver twins to a dear family in Eufaula.

In Slocomb, an abundant tomato crop proved too much for the local packing shed workers, so the Alabama angels helped ready the tomatoes for shipment.

Homecoming at a small country church went without a hitch after the Alabama angels pitched in to do the last minute chores when the preacher got the flu.

Bringing a wished-for
puppy to a little Tuskegee boy
delighted them as they
watched his happy face from
behind a cloud.

When the Lord told
Bubba that they could escort
the New Year to Opp, their
wings puffed with pride.

Scottsboro was in a quandary. A late frost had ruined the Easter lilies that were to be used for sunrise services.

Sara and Emily gathered Heaven's finest and, with the help of the others, they had them in place for a glorious Easter Morning.

Meanwhile, Bubba helped the bluebird practice his song.

"We know that God makes all things work together for the good of those who love God." (Rom. 8:28). So during the year the opportunities for the Alabama angels to do the Lord's work were numerous.

Christmas is the favorite time of the year for all angels. The Alabama angels delight in finding a special family with a new baby boy. They bring him gifts of love and song to celebrate the birth of Baby Jesus so many years ago. They may be in a rural Alabama community or in metropolitan Montgomery or Birmingham. The excitement is the same because they have the pleasure of honoring the Lord as the angels did in Bethlehem.

Wherever you are in the State of Alabama, when the moon is high in the Southern sky, in the hush of the night you might hear the flutter of wings and the tiptoe of tiny feet. Look carefully and believe.

You will see the glow of magic haloes as they light the way of the Alabama angels.

The End